To Oscar and Leo
S.B.

First published in North America in 2018 by Boxer Books Limited.

www.boxerbooks.com

Boxer® is a registered trademark of Boxer Books Limited

Text and illustrations copyright © 2018 Sebastien Braun
The rights of Sebastien Braun to be identified as the author
and illustrator of this work have been asserted by him
in accordance with the Copyright, Designs and Patents Act, 1988.

The illustrations were prepared in mixed media.

Library-of-Congress Cataloging-in-Publication Data available.

ISBN 978-1-910716-30-4

1 3 5 7 9 10 8 6 4 2

Printed in China

All of our papers are sourced from managed forests
and renewable resources.

I Love My
BABY

Sebastien Braun

Boxer Books

I kiss my baby
every morning.

I give my babies
food to eat.

I bring my babies
sweet surprises.

I love to take
my baby sailing.

I teach my babies
to swim at the pond.

When it rains
I like taking
long naps
with my baby.

I love it when my
babies run to me.

I watch
my baby
play in
the forest.

I keep my baby
cozy and warm.

I love to
sing songs
with
my baby.

I give my baby
big snuggly hugs.

I love my baby.